©1997 Annick Press Ltd. (North American edition)
©1996 Éditions du Seuil (original edition)
Original edition *Beaux Dimanches*, published by Seuil Jeunesse, France.
All rights reserved. Annick Press Ltd.
Distributed in North America by Firefly Books Ltd. Willowdale, ON   M2H 3K1

Printed in Belgium

Cataloguing in Publication Data

Pratt, Pierre
  [Beaux dimanches. English]
  Hippo Beach

North American ed.

Translation of: Beaux dimanches.

ISBN 1-55037-419-2

I. Title. II. Title: Beaux dimanches. English.

PS8581.R377B4313 1997   jC813'.54   C96-990066-X
PZ7.P72Hi 1997

Hippo Beach

Pierre Pratt

Annick Press Ltd.
Toronto • New York

Today is Sunday.

And already, Jeff is dreaming about next Sunday.